THE
SERPENT'S STAR

MURIAL ROBERTSON 1

By Sarah Ickes

•

Originally Published
October 2021

•

A Historical Mystery Series

YOU WILL BE HUNTED DOWN
LIKE THE PREY YOU ONCE
THOUGHT ME OF
- THE SERPENT

JULY 1886

Murial Robertson................... main character, works for her father on his security team

Jack Fulton............................. sheriff of Conestone

Curt Ruger.............................. chief deputy sheriff of Conestone

Walter Crancin....................... bank manager, Murial's cousin

Senator Gerald Robertson...... senator campaigning for Arizona to be a state, Murial's father

Clive Johnson.......................... senator's campaign manager

Brewer..................................... man with a well-groomed mustache

and....

You will have to read on to learn about the others!

The sun glinted off of the tin metal star she held in her hand as it soaked up the overwhelming heat. She longed for the cooler environment she had grown up with on the east coast, but acknowledged that the dry heat, distinguishing this part of the country as a place all its own, was far better than the saturating humidity of her home. Studying her new surroundings, the five foot six inches tall woman watched the people milling about the activity-filled streets. Dust clouds swarmed around their feet and danced into the air before vanishing without a trace. Her eyes were alert and sharp, being the exact reason for her father's trust in her, to scout out the road ahead of him while campaigning along the trails.

Being an artist gave her an edge in paying attention to the minute details that saved her father's life on more than one occasion. It wasn't heard of to have a female scout on a Senator's security detail, and the very notion challenged the social structure of the times. Her job, however, was not a blessing, but rather a curse in disguise.

This town seemed like all the rest at first appearance - stocked with saloons, gambling houses, and few reputable shops for the people of Conestone in the territory of Arizona. Drunken cowboys sleeping it off in the alleys, or puking up the previous night's festivities in a disgusting sobering process, dotted the side streets.

As her fingers toyed with the metal star in her hand, she rubbed it mindlessly with her full attention focused on where her father should make his speeches. Her sturdy figure was hidden by her big belled dress and its dark blue drapery with ruffles. A baby blue parasol hung off her left arm and she neatly opened the laced fabric before leaning the rod against her left shoulder. Producing a smile on her wrinkle-free face, she daintily dipped her head to the stunned cowboys that parted the seas for her to walk down the sidewalk unimpeded.

Some of the gambling girls were whistling, jealous at her flauntingly wealthy attire, but she took the distasteful remarks in stride, and continued toward the center of town. She felt a sense of renewal after being able to freshen up at the hotel from a long and filthy journey by means of the stagecoach. While the scenery was quite beautiful between the variety of cacti and saguaro, the dusty winds and cramped quarters on the stagecoach was not her idea of a good time. The only pleasures she obtained from her trips was learning about the other travelers' experiences and from the artistic inspirations nature had to offer. Even as she was walking down the street, her mind could not stop studying the way the light and shadows were playing off one another. It was not long until her destination appeared on her right and she heard the creaking from the wood under her feet where she stopped.

The local bank was a single-story brick building with small glass pane windows and minimal decor inside the main lobby. She walked in through the front door to find the only teller helping an elderly gentleman make his deposit at the wooden counter with metal bars separating them. Two minutes later, the brown door to her right opened and a rotund gentleman, dressed in a brown suit, eagerly motioned at her to join him. Obligingly, the lady placed her parasol back onto her arm and walked through the threshold into a small office with one window that watched over the mountains in the distance. Several nearby farms dotted the landscape with moving shadows casting downward from the crawling clouds above. Sitting in the chair facing his pine wooden desk, she waited for the middle-aged man with glasses to take his seat. "You're looking as good as ever, Murial. Have not seen you in a long time. I was surprised to find out that your father sent you ahead of him instead of one of his security men." His tenor-like voice briefly added to the clock ticking endlessly away at the back of the room, hanging above cabinets over-stuffed with paperwork.

"It is so good to see you too, cousin." Murial didn't realize that her right hand was still playing with the Sheriff's star until she stood up to give him a hug, pricking him in the process. Her cousin shifted his gaze to the pin and she quickly stashed it into a hip pocket within the fold of her dress, along with a quickly spoken apology. She awkwardly gulped down some saliva in her throat and patted the pocket with her hand while looking at the worn-out floorboards between her feet.

"You still have Uncle Seb's star? He always did seem to favor you." He was perplexed by the shame written on her face. "Did I say something wrong already?"

Murial appreciated his attempt to lighten her mood with some humor. "No, not at all. I just…it's just that… well, I guess I should be over his passing by now."

"Don't be ashamed that you still miss him, Murial. If your father is the one feeding you that nonsense - why, he is the reason that you grew so close with Uncle Seb." His attention was redirected to the pencil in his hand, rubbing the smooth sides in rhythm, catching himself before he went too far in consoling her. Sweat ran down his slightly tanned, rounded face and he sighed awkwardly as he padded his forehead dry with a handkerchief that had been tucked away in his pants pocket. He leaned his body weight against the table. "So, how long have you been here?"

Murial's eyes shifted back onto the star's new location for a moment before replying. "What do you think? A waste of time or not?" Her style had always been more direct than what most of the women in her social status were expected to behave like, but that never stopped her. Ever since childhood, she had possessed a more factual demeanor and truth in her words as opposed to the idle gossip typically exchanged among the genteel. Always sneaking her way into her father's office to hear the political talks and war statistics landed her mind in a more knowledgeable place, however, it also placed her butt in more than a few spankings.

"To the point as always. Some things never change." Her cousin's mouth smiled from only one corner as he continued. "I think it is worth a shot, but I can't guarantee anything." Murial's eyes flashed hard as rocks toward her cousin and her voice spouted out daggers upon hearing his answer. Surprisingly, her cousin did not seem taken aback by her sudden turn of mood.

"Worth a shot?! Walter, my father is risking a lot for this campaign and we need to know if coming here would be worth it or not!" Murial shot up from the uncomfortable chair to pace around the room, anger fuming inside her. "He is putting pressure on me like you would not believe. Telling me to keep this tour moving steadily along so he is in a location no more than a week to eliminate any..." Her mouth clammed up tight when she realized what was about to slip from her lips.

"Where is he now?"

"Hacksaw, two weeks away. I have been trying to keep ahead of schedule, but a tornado took out one of the towns and there is time for only one more location before heading onto California. It is either here in Conestone or over in Burkville." Murial's focus stopped on a landscape painting sitting beside the clock, counting away the seconds like grains of sand through a sieve.

"Burkville? They do not care about anything that isn't related to farming and could care less about becoming a state. Why, half of their population is made up of bandits hiding from the law."

"I know, but my father's campaign manager stupidly suggested it and has been persistent at making sure he gets there as his final stop. A little too persistent if you ask me. That is why I need evidence that coming here would be better than going to Burkville. I haven't liked Clive from the start, but I have a feeling that there is something more behind his decision. However, when I bring it up with my stubborn father, he does not wish to hear a single bad word against his 'friend' and the conversation ends with him shouting for me to stop contradicting him." Her eyes squinted, gazing at the painting and the strokes used to create the life-like imitation. It had been some time since her hand had created it. Even so, she remembered the strokes like it was yesterday.

Walter sensed a longing in her stare, despite only seeing the back of her head, and his face saddened with the possible reality she could have been living. If Murial wasn't his cousin, he would have asked her to marry him when they were teenagers back East. Her passion for art and life was unmatched by any other woman he had ever met and he pitied her current situation. "How has your artwork been

5

going?"

Murial's outstretched hand, toward her initials on the painting, halted abruptly and she snapped back to the task at present. Her watery eyes were steadfast; but, she did not turn around as she spoke. "Fine."

Her lips tightened as she moved slowly through the small room and over to the only window displaying the true countryside. She fought back her long internal struggle, wanting desperately to confide in her cousin, but remaining as quiet as ever instead. Uncle Seb, Walter, and her grandmother were the only family she had felt a true kinship towards. Their uncle was another rebel of the family, and encouraged her to be herself in opposition to society's imposed boundaries. Senator Robertson, her father, was not of his brother's mindset. Rather he was of the status quo, and forced Murial into this position to silence her artistic desires. His claim was that he was already risking enough, politically, by having her in his security detail.

"He hasn't accepted your art dream has he?" Walter's eyes grew compassionate toward his cousin, who possessed the talent and drive of a professional artist if her gender was that of a man. That was something he always admired about Murial; that despite society being ever so against her gender, she didn't let it stand in her way. At least, that is how he had always known her to be. But the woman standing in front of him was not the same one he had left back home four years ago.

"He has me doing this job, and is paying me fair wages, so I am not to complain." Murial recited her father's words like a script in a play and wanted to change the topic all together. "So far, I have been in town for three hours and I believe that the two trees by the stream, at the edge of town, would be the safest location to house my father's speeches."

"By Old Man Boris's land? What's wrong with having it in town? Or the Dance Hall for that matter?"

Murial shook her head. "No good. Too many high vantage points from the multiple two-story buildings and the Dance Hall has too many possible exits to cover. Besides, I have seen all of the sealed mine shafts throughout the streets. The leftover tunnels from past mine explorations are too numerous to count. No, outside of town is best." She kept staring out the window, watching the sunlight cast short shadows from its high noon position.

Walter didn't give up trying. "What about the church? It is a short distance from the other buildings."

Murial turned around and looked at her cousin in disbelief. "Do you honestly think that my father would do that?"

Walter chuckled. "You do know your stuff, I will say that. But what about one of the saloons? I just think that you would be better off with a location in town if you want a better turnout." Her cousin was one of few people not scared off by Murial's authoritative stature and personality.

"Then we can take the liquor to them by the stream, but it is my father's life that is on the line here and I say it isn't safe for him to be a standing target." Her dress swished slightly as she stepped up to Walter, who took his turn at studying her for clues as to what was making her so testy. Reading people was not his strong suit, but he did have a suspicion that she was trying to hang on to what little she had left in terms of a life under constant scrutiny from her oppressive father.

"Whatever has your father spooked must be serious. I don't know of too many people who scare him." Walter grabbed both ends of his pencil and snapped it in half with ease. Everything always seemed to be about his Uncle the Senator when it came to family matters, like he was the only son his grandfather ever had who amounted to anything; despite having two other sons and two daughters. His mother was the third born and the eldest daughter. So her family was not seen upon with much favor from their grandfather. His grandmother, on the other hand, adored them along with Murial and their kinship was closer than most.

"You have no idea." Murial spoke with her eyes distantly in the past. Her gaze wandered back to her cousin as she bid him farewell. "I must go and speak with the sheriff across the street to hear his opinion before contacting my father. Shall we have dinner tonight at the hotel?"

Walter's lips quivered and his forehead was perspiring again. "Well, yes, but um…"

"Say 6:30?" Murial was fiddling with her parasol and not paying attention to Walter's nervous expressions.

"Yes, that will be fine. But Murial, there is something I need to tell you…"

"You can tell me at dinner, Walter." Murial's hand grabbed the doorknob to leave when Walter suddenly gripped onto her wrist in protest. Her eyes slowly moved from his hand and up towards his eyes. "Walter, you still have a hand because of who you are. But, if you do not remove it in the next ten seconds, it will not matter whether you are my cousin or not."

"Fine, I am not going to tell you. But, hear me out. Do not overreact."

"Why would I?" Murial's face displayed her curiosity, but Walter just removed his hand calmly and graciously opened the door for her. She eyed him on her way out and dipped her head to the cowboy holding the front door open for her as she exited the bank. *I wonder what that was all about?*

The sun was unrelenting in its hold on the town and

Murial's body instantly began sweating from underneath all her clothing. Her corset felt just the tiniest bit tighter with each breath. She waited for a passing stagecoach before walking across the street and onto the sidewalk in front of the sheriff's office. Murial's attention was too preoccupied with brushing her dress off from the dusty street, to make a good first impression, that she failed to see the name painted on the sheriff's sign before walking through the front door.

A slender man dressed in a cowhide vest over his red shirt and tan pants stood in the middle of the room with paperwork in his hands. One look at Murial and he dipped his hat in greeting, fumbling with a nearby chair while still managing to awkwardly hold onto his papers.

"Ma'am. Won't you have a seat?"

She could tell that he was a southern man by his accent. "Are you the sheriff?"

"Why no, the sheriff is out catching a runaway prisoner, but he shouldn't be long."

"How do you know he will not be long?"

"Well, Scott has a bum leg and isn't sober yet. He gets drunk almost every weekend he is in town, and well, let's just say he ain't too bright."

Murial raised her eyebrows in understanding. "Oh, I see. And you are?"

"My name is Curt Ruger, Ma'am, and I am the Chief Deputy Sheriff. Pleased to meet you Miss…"

"Miss Robertson. Likewise Mr. Ruger. If it's alright with you, I think I will just wait for the sheriff here."

"Be my guest, Miss Robertson." He gestured toward the chair he just pulled out from in front of his desk on the right side of the room, and Murial took him up on his offer. She patted her parasol down on top of her lap and made some idle chit-chat with the Deputy Sheriff until a horse was heard from outside, about ten minutes later. Curt headed out to greet the Sheriff and their prisoner, Scott, while Murial tucked in a stray strand of hair that had fallen in front of her eyes and patiently waited. Curt dragged Scott through the door and toward the back jail cells, giving him a half-hearted scolding for trying to escape.

She watched as the sheriff walked in from the dusty outside and removed his hat to beat his clothes clean from his dirt covered body. Murial's face widened in shock and disbelief as the dust settled and the man went over to the water pitcher located atop his desk, on the left side of the room. Her mouth hung open as she stood up from the chair the moment Curt finished locking Scott away. "By the way Jack, this lady would like to see you about something." His arm motioned in Murial's direction. The parasol slid from her grip and collided onto the ground with a small thud.

Jack turned around and his face told her that he recognized her. He walked excitedly over to her frozen body. "Murial Robertson! It is so good to see you!" He reached out to give her a friendly bear hug, as if they were old friends. Her mouth closed and her eyes were stern but she reciprocated his welcome with a handshake instead.

"Jack Fulton. Never thought I would ever see you again."

He looked into her dark brown eyes. "Same stern look you always had for me. Some things don't get better with age, huh?"

"Well, how did you think I would treat you after all the boot-licking you did to my father?"

"Nah, you are just jealous because you were the only girl on our street I didn't court at one time or another." Jack's equally brown eyes lit up as he brushed his right hand through his dark hair, plastered with sweat and filth, over his sunbaked face.

"You always did think that everything was about

you." Murial rolled her eyes and placed her hand on her hip. "Look, I am not here to reminisce. I am here for an important matter."

"I had a feeling it was not because you missed me." His smile was smirking and playful in its meaning.

"Oh, wind up, will you? I need to talk to you about my father possibly visiting Conestone in a fortnight as part of his campaigning for this territory to become a state." Murial reached down to grab her parasol that had fallen to the floor. Jack's face grew a bit more serious.

"I was wondering why you were dressed up. Even back home you refused to be seen with a parasol. That is your disguise isn't it?" Murial glanced down at the parasol in her hands and shamefully slipped it behind her back, dropping it onto the chair. Her face betrayed the answer. "So he sends you, the unexpected dainty daughter ahead, to scout things out so as to not arouse suspicion. Is that right?" Jack leaned back against his desk, studying her body language. "You do realize that you stick out worse than a pink flower in a green field around these parts?"

"I know that. If anyone asks, I am on my way to California to meet up with some relatives that have gone on ahead of me."

"Is even part of that true?" Jack raised an eyebrow. Murial took a step closer to him.

"Isn't truth the best lie?"

She hadn't aged much since the last day he had seen her, three years, five months, and twenty days ago. He had memorized her sweet face with light pink lips and her unruly hair she loved to let run wild. The story in her eyes gave away the lapse of time, hardened but not stone, and her stare was strong but gentle.

"I am here to get your opinion first before reporting back to him. He is two weeks away and I have to send him a

telegram tonight before his mind is made up by Clive."
Murial was restraining her pride in having to stoop to ask for
Jack's help.

"Your father is still with that weasel as his campaign
manager?" Jack shook his head. "Well, I guess that means
that good ole Clive wants your father to go somewhere else
to do his campaigning and you are trying to persuade him
otherwise." Murial nodded her head in agreement and Jack
continued. "I'm not sure that many people in this town
would care much about this area becoming a state, but you
have a right to try. Why ask me? Does he not have his own
bodyguards?"

"He does, but we make it a policy to let the law
know ahead of time before coming into town so we can coo-
perate together." Murial stated flatly. Jack was not
convinced.

"I know you Murial, and that was not you talking.
Your father has you trained well to spit out his lies."

Murial's blood was hot and pumping loud as her
hands turned into fists. "See here you pompous Lunk-head!
My father sent me here to scout out the town upon my
request because Clive wants to head to Burkville. I didn't
know you were the Sheriff here, but if my father's life was
not on the line, I would be out this door in an instant. Now,
are you going to help me or not?"

Jack's head cocked to one side. "Your father that
fearful for his life? It must be serious if he is that scared.
Then why doesn't he just turn around and go home?"

Murial was becoming extremely impatient. "You
really think my father would do that?!" She turned her back
to him and fetched her parasol before heading toward the
door. Jack reached out and grabbed her arm.

"Where are you going?"

Murial glared back at him. "To the hotel, if you

do not mind. Or are you going to arrest me for something?"

He backed away from her and softened his approach. "That is fine with me. I was just asking." Rubbing his fingers down the side of his hat, Jack was trying to decide if he should ask her a particular question. "Hey, do you want to have dinner tonight? It's on me."

"No thank you. I already have plans for dinner." Murial turned and stormed out of the office and into the dusty Monday afternoon.

Walter was happy to be able to talk to Murial while eating dinner in her hotel room. "This is quite nice and more peaceful than being at Molly's with everyone chatting up a storm."

"I am sorry, Walter. It's just that I have become so used to eating in my room due to my father's position, that I find it hard to go back to eating in public." Murial's gaze fell to her food as her fork picked at the chicken on her plate.

"No, it was a compliment, really. I find this a nice change. How did your meeting with Jack go?" Walter was unsure on whether he should have asked after seeing Murial beginning to fume once more.

"It was definitely a surprise, I can tell you that. And it did not go all that well."

"He really isn't that bad once you get to know him Murial."

"Are you still defending him? Walter, he is a Boot-Lick. Always agreeing with my father, like a lap dog would, and helping him with his work and…" Murial shook the rest of the statement away from her mind. "I am not going to talk about it." Walter decided to change the subject and asked her if she had reported back to her father as of yet. "No, I have not. Because, I am not sure what I am going to do. Even Jack says that the effort might not lead anywhere. I just do not know Walter. I was hoping to find something here that would force my father to change his mind about Burkville. I have had my reservations about Clive before, but something is not adding up this time. I was just at Burkville yesterday and it is about the same as here."

"You were in Burkville by yourself?! Murial, I am surprised that you were not kidnapped, or worse." Walter's voice lowered as if someone might be listening in on their conversation.

"I was not alone. There were some very nice people on the stage and I ended up befriending an older Colonel on his way to California. He escorted me around the town for a couple of days and I thanked him by paying his ticket to San Francisco." Murial shoved some chicken and potatoes into her mouth. "And I will have to tell you, Walter, for all the frightful stories that are spread about that town, I almost think it is better there than it is here." Her face smiled when the comment riled her cousin up, just as she expected it would.

"Now, that isn't true. We have some good folks here from back East that do care and are willing to listen. I trust your judgment, Murial, and so does your father. Send him a telegram in the morning explaining as such and make him listen." Walter shoved more mashed potatoes into his mouth as three knocks came from the door. Murial rose from the wooden chair and walked past the bed and nightstand to open the door with two gunshot holes by the knob. Her eyes rolled once again when she saw Jack standing there, cleaned up from the afternoon's pursuit and grinning from ear to ear.

"May I come in?"

"Sure thing Jack. There is plenty of food." Walter did not give Murial a chance to refuse him entry and Jack slipped in past her.

"Boy, that food smells good. Is it from Molly's?"

The two men laughed and talked like Murial wasn't even there and she slipped back into her seat, silent and unamused. It was not until Jack had his plate filled with Molly's food that he spoke in Murial's direction. "You can't allow your father to go to Burkville." He stuffed his mouth and watched Murial's interest grow from his peripheral vision. "I contacted the sheriff there by telegram and he informed me that there have been some strangers slowly coming into town over the past week."

"That does not mean anything." Murial returned to her dinner.

"No, but they are being very secretive and one of them happens to be a known gunfighter. His wanted poster is hanging in my office."

"Why does the sheriff not arrest him?" Walter inquired.

"Because he has a feeling that something bigger is brewing. So he has asked for some United States Deputies to come in." Jack eyed the satisfied look on Murial's face. Once she spotted him watching her, her face hardened again.

"Well, that is great news, huh Murial?" Walter pointed his fork at her. "That gives you something to use in persuading your father." Murial's face slightly softened.

"Yes, it does. I cannot believe I'm saying this, but thank you Jack."

"You are quite welcome, Miss Robertson."

Walter checked the time by his pocket watch and dabbed his mouth with his napkin. "Well, I hate to end such a lovely evening, but I must be going. I have work in the morning." Murial's eyes lit up.

"You still have the pocket watch I gave you for Christmas?"

"Why, of course. It did come from my favorite cousin." Walter winked at Murial and bid them farewell as he headed out the door. Silence fell after the door shut with only the sound of Jack's eating audible and Murial's hand rubbing over her Uncle's star under the table. The metal had somewhat cooled from the day's heat, smooth and calming with each stroke of her thumb.

Jack looked over at her to find Murial staring at a distant place and time. "I am really sorry about what happened to your uncle."

"You were there for the funeral and had spoken your condolences then. Anyway, it was over three years ago." Her hand stopped in mid-stroke.

"I realize that. But I also know how much he meant to you. Despite the fact that time has since moved on, the pain does not."

"What would you know about it?" Murial challenged him with her glare and threw her uncle's star onto the table. "You are a man living in a man's world with everything at your disposal. My Uncle Seb was one of the few that believed in me and challenged me to strive for better. He supported me going after my dream of being an artist and selling my artwork instead of becoming a housewife, knowing that that kind of life would hollow me from the inside out." She stood abruptly from the table and moved away from her chair. Jack rested his fork down upon his folded napkin.

"I may not know what it is like for you, but I do know about pain and rejection." Jack removed himself from the table. "Thank you for the dinner." Without another word, he walked over to the door and let himself out. Murial was confused by his statement and sat on the end of the bed in thought for a time. The next thing she knew, her eyes were closed and she was back home on the worst day of her life.

It was New Year's Eve, three years ago, and Jack was downstairs with her father as usual. Murial was sitting on the balcony outside her bedroom and was painting with the paints and brushes her uncle had given to her for Christmas. Shannon, her sister, had helped her stretch a roll of canvas over a frame she constructed under her grandmother's guidance and was happily filling it with vibrant colors. Upon hearing her name being bellowed from her father, she reluctantly headed down the hall and staircase.

"I have heard from your mother that you have decided not to go to the Henrys' tonight for the ball?!" Senator Robertson shouted at her.

Murial was defiant and rigid. "Yes, that would be correct, Father."

"That is unacceptable. You have twenty minutes to get ready. Shannon, go help your sister!" Shannon hesitated as she looked between the two, not wanting to be caught in the middle of their argument.

"That will not be necessary Shannon, because I am not going." Murial turned and headed back up the stairs toward her bedroom with her father raging behind her.

"THIS IS ALL MY BROTHER'S DOING! TURNING YOU AGAINST ME!" He stormed after her and pushed Murial out of the way once they reached her bedroom. She screamed while her horrified eyes watched her father draw a knife from his pocket and slashed through her painting.

Tears streamed down her face as all the anger inside

propelled her forward and she attacked him like a wild man. The Senator simply shoved her aside and she landed on her bed, crying. "If you will not go to the ball tonight, then you shall not paint either. Why can you not be more like your sister or Jack? The sooner you learn that I am running this show, the better it will be for you."

Murial shriveled on her bed as sorrow filled her heart. The Senator thrust his knife back into his pocket and strutted down the stairs. Her grief consumed her so much so that she failed to hear the sound of footsteps approaching her room. Only when Jack had reached her bedside did she feel his presence and turned around, trying to blink away the tears in order to see the person standing there.

His hand was outstretched while holding a single lilac, her favorite flower, with a compassionate smile. Her hand flew at the flower and struck it on the ground. "I will never be like you!" Murial stated and turned her back to him.

The light streamed upon her face and woke her from her sleep. Her eyes flashed open at the same instant gunshots rang out from the street below and the glass in her hotel room window shattered. She rolled onto the floor and held her head down while listening to the feet of chaos running up and down the hallway. Shouting and more shots were filling the morning air and she remained hunkered down for the next five minutes. Murial raised her head when the noise dissipated but she changed her mind again when there was a knock on her door.

"Miss Robertson, it's Chief Deputy Ruger. Are you alright?" Curt spoke through the locked door. Murial picked herself up and dusted off her dress, appalled that she had fallen asleep in her day outfit. She opened the door and let Curt inside.

"Yes, I am alright. However, I can't say the same for my window." Murial pointed toward the broken glass fragments lying on the floor.

"Oh, I'll have Bert come around to patch it up for you Ma'am. But I am sure glad that you're alright." Curt dipped his hat to Murial and she nodded in return.

"Why thank you Curt. That was very nice of you to check up on me."

Curt gave her a sideways glance while he kicked some of the glass into a pile with his boots. "It wasn't me Ma'am. It was Jack that sent me over to check on you." Murial's face widened with surprise.

"What was all the noise about anyways?"

"Just a few cowhands wanting to stir up some trouble. It's like a land war out here. But Jack got them under control and Deputy Harrison is taking them back to jail while Jack gets looked at by the Doc."

Murial's attention was grabbed immediately. "Is he okay?"

"Right as rain. Just hit him in the arm and luckily not his gun arm." Curt eyed her with a sly smile and Murial retracted her interest.

"My uncle was a sheriff and passed away when someone shot him in the chest. I am just glad that Sheriff Fulton will be alright." Murial thanked Curt again and ushered him out of her room. She rapidly gathered herself together and headed down to the telegraph office hidden inside the stagecoach depot.

"Excuse me, I would like to send a telegram, please." Murial greeted the elderly clerk, who obliged and she paid him after sending her father her report. She asked him directions to the doctor's office and hastily made her way down the street and to the left of the tree by the stables where Walter was already waiting outside the doctor's door.

"Good Morning, Murial. Curt told me that a couple of the shots were fired into your room from this morning's events. Are you okay?"

"Yes, I'm fine. Curt informed me that Jack received a bullet in the arm. I just came from the telegraph office to see how he was doing."

"Better than the other fellas." Jack opened the door with his left arm in a sling. "If I would have known it would have taken getting shot to have you come and see me, I would have gotten shot sooner." Walter chuckled and gave him a pat on his good arm.

"Glad to see your sense of humor is still intact."

Murial resisted the urge to give him her normally steely glare. "It was very nice of you to send Curt over to check in on me. You did not have to do that."

"Nonsense. Walter's my friend and he would kill me if anything was to happen to you." Jack's look was sincere and Murial allowed a small smile to form on her lips.

Walter's gaze shifted back and forth between them for a moment before excusing himself back to the bank. "I'm glad to hear that you are alright buddy and I am sure that Murial has a few things she will need to discuss with you after her father decides to visit."

"You sent him the telegram?"

"I did. I just hope that he agrees with my decision. No telling what that slimy Clive has put into his mind." Jack and Murial walked beside one another back toward the hotel. "You don't have to walk me back to my hotel room, Jack."

"It is the polite thing to do. Besides, it isn't often that I get to walk with the most beautiful woman in town." Jack noticed the smile on Murial's face. "That makes two smiles I have gotten out of you today. That is a record for me, considering that you have never smiled at me before."

"You have not gotten shot before. At least that I know of, so there are some exceptions."

Jack's expression turned more serious in nature. "I never told you this, but your uncle was the one who inspired me to become a Sheriff."

Murial stopped dead in her tracks and looked at Jack with bewilderment. "But you were always so enamored with my father and the politics of Washington." She watched him study the dirt as he was about to say something when Curt approached them.

"Sorry to interrupt Jack, but you are needed out at Rendson's farm. Karen is in your office. Looks like this bunch was a distraction for us while the others are surrounding Paul's house." Jack excused himself and Murial was left in suspense of what he was on the verge of saying. She watched the two men walk down the street, discussing what the situation was according to Karen's account.

As Murial made her way back to the hotel, she caught a glimpse of a man lurking in the shadows of the alleyway. Her attentive stare caused the man to flee and Murial thought better of chasing after him. Shaking off a feeling of curiosity, she reached the door of the hotel to find the lobby half-filled with stranded travelers. The clerk at the counter was trying to handle the grumblings from the dissatisfied customers. Even though his voice was barely holding any authoritative presence, the clerk did his best.

"Now, ladies and gentlemen, I know that this is not what you had planned, but the company is paying for your hotel room while they fix the stage."

While navigating her way through the crowd, Murial overheard two older women gabbing about an engagement announcement they would be attending in California. The one lady still had some black hair mixed in with her upcoming gray and lowered her voice to a whisper. "Wait, what do you mean he has not asked her yet?"

"I mean just that - he has not asked her yet. I do not know why my boy has sent for us, I just do not know. Apparently he says that the deal is done." The other lady had a completely white head of hair and wore fashion more suitable for one of the cities back East. Murial tried to get a good look at the women without causing a stir, but she was ultimately swept up in the directional flow of the group wandering toward the stairs. She was happy to have some personal space once again after shutting the door to her room behind her. *That must be what a cow feels like in a corral,* Murial thought to herself.

The air was warming up outside so she retrieved some sketching materials from her trunk to make good use of the beautiful day. With the pencil resting familiarly in her hand, she sat by the window to draw inspiration from the landscape before her. Two pages of sketches and ideas were filled by the time a knock was heard from the door. Walter walked in, upon her admittance, and his eyes lit up when he saw what she had been up too. "Your drawings are always so well done."

Murial's cheeks blushed slightly at his praise. "Thank you."

His eyes were attempting to search her face for an answer to his question before saying it aloud. "Did he tell you?"

"Tell me what?" Murial was perplexed as to what her cousin was referring to.

Walter suddenly became embarrassed and hastily shoved the subject under the rug. "Sorry, I thought he told you. The way you two were actually getting along today… by the way, where is Jack?" She informed him of what she knew about the situation out at Rendson's farm. Walter shook his head, "There is so much war and dispute over land out here. When are people going to learn that there is enough to go around? Why do some men have to be so greedy?"

"I don't know, Walter. Now, what has Jack not told me?" Murial tried, and failed, to get her cousin to spill the beans. Walter left the room with his hat in his hands, speed-walking down the hall before she could think about chasing after him.

Murial ate alone that evening, listening to the woman, in the next room, sing a song about the South. Her voice was soothing in a sad but pleasing manner, and she listened to it while reading over her father's response to her telegram. The hotel clerk had delivered it with her food and even though her father's response was in her favor, she was not as thrilled by her victory as she had expected to be. Traveling was the one aspect of her job she enjoyed, and discovering new experiences without being under the control of her hot-tempered father. Whenever he came, her life would have to be put on hold to suit his purposes once again and as time ticked on, Murial found it increasingly harder to keep up the fake pretenses that Clive choreographed for them.

Lying on the bed, she felt consumed by the memories she had of her father condemning her, shouting at her, guilting her for being who she was inside. Darkness was closing in and she desperately wanted to curl up tighter than a ball, crying herself to sleep. Her rounded cheeks were stained with tears and she placed the paper on the nightstand through blurry eyes.

The nightgown she unearthed from her clothes, swayed around her body while she slowly strolled across the room and to the still broken window. Murial looked up to see the moon as a thin crescent in the sky, mirroring itself within her eyes watered by sorrow.

Jack's nerves were causing his body to wriggle like a floundering fish out of water. Walter had bet him five dollars that he wouldn't have the guts to tell Murial the truth. Despite seeing his friend's good intentions, Jack cursed him for putting him in this situation. Curt had also joined in on the fun and took Walter up on the bet, then told Jack that he owed him one for getting them out of a sticky jam with some gunfighters a year back. "Some friends... acting like matchmakers!" Jack grumbled. He cleared his throat and was about to place his knuckles on the door when it flew open backwards. Murial was caught off guard by his presence at her doorway.

"Morning, Murial. I was wondering if you would like some breakfast at Molly's?" Jack's mouth fumbled at a smile, which vexed Murial even further.

"I have never seen you so clumsy at trying to get a girl. It took traveling thousands of miles for you to try it on me, huh?" She tried concealing her amusement. Something was telling her to take him up on his offer, but she felt the past scraping away at her mind. "Thank you, but no. I have an important date with a tree."

"A what?" Jack was both deflated and intrigued by her response.

"But, if you have time to be a model, I guess you can join me…" She forced a smile once her face was out of his view. *There, I am trying to be nice.* They walked out to the two trees by the stream and she instructed him on where to stand, positioning him leaning against the tree trunk with his face turned in the opposite direction of his body. She paced back a couple of feet and began to sketch. After roughly ten minutes transpired, Jack broke the silence.

"So, what have you been up to lately?"

"Do not move your head." Murial continued for a few moments before responding. "This job. Other than that, trying to keep up my art in contrast to certain aspects of life's wishes."

"In other words, your father." Jack watched her stoic reaction out of the corner of his eye.

"What? You already have a medal. Waiting for another one for your "clever deductions?" Murial sarcastically stated.

"If you carry so much disdain for him, why do you stay?"

"Do we have to talk about him?" An edge of hostility was growing in her voice.

"I'm trying to understand. That is all."

Murial sighed, "Leave it be. If you are going to continue asking bothersome questions, feel free to leave."

"But then you will not have a model. Isn't it the humans within a piece of art that give it intrigue?" Jack turned his head and watched her expression with some satisfaction that his statement had grabbed her full attention.

"Do not tell me that you actually remember me saying that?" Murial's hand stopped in mid-stroke on the paper and locked eyes with him. This was the door that Jack had been waiting for and he seized his chance.

"Maybe…see, there was this girl I once knew. She loved art…and she was very skilled and talented. This girl fascinated me and I wished to be with her, learning more about the way she thought and saw the world. But, her father was a tyrant and kept his family on tight ropes." Jack began walking up to her while he explained. "So, I tried what I could to see her, speak to her, and when the time came that I might finally have the chance to court her, she turned me down harder than I could ever have imagined." She gasped as her mind was filling in the puzzle while he continued. "You see, it wasn't your father I was enamored with Murial."

"I knew that your father would not let me near you unless I got to know him first. So I said all the right things and did what he asked to gain his favor, so that I might ask him for permission to court you. When the timing seemed about right, he asked me if I liked Shannon and started arranging it so that we would spend time together. I felt trapped because I did not care for Shannon the same way I cared for you, but I did not want to upset your father and take away any chance I had. So I ended up talking with your sister and explained the situation to her. She also felt the same way about me and had agreed to help. But then, New Year's Eve happened."

Murial's eyes widened with realization. "I struck your hand away that night because I was too upset over what my father had done." Jack nodded.

"We all heard him from below. That is why I headed up with the flower I was going to surprise you with at the ball. Your father pushed me into the coach with the rest of your family and we headed to the Henrys' for the dance."

"That is why you left the next day? My mother and I

always wondered why you had just disappeared into thin air. I asked Shannon about it once, but she refused to tell me."

"I could not take any more of what your father was doing to you and what he did by poisoning you against me. So I had it out with him and told him everything. He said that if I truly cared for you I would leave and never come back or else you would pay the price. So, I left and joined Walter out here in Conestone." Murial didn't know what to say. All the resentment and anger she held against Jack seemed silly and shameful all of a sudden.

"Why did you not tell me?" She challenged, trying to console herself that she was not a fool for the way she had acted these past years.

"You know how your father is, Murial. He is good at controlling your family's lives. And it hasn't been so bad out here. I get to do what your uncle did." Jack smiled and looked into Murial's softened gaze.

She moved toward him, about to lean inward before dodging away and grabbing her things in a hurry. "I must be going." Jack watched with despair as she headed for the hotel, not looking back to see him watching her rejection for the second time. When she reached her hotel room, Murial nearly slipped on the note that had been shoved under the door, lying over a crevice in the floorboards. Since it had been given to her in such an underhanded manner, she assumed that the sender did not wish to be seen by the clerk and opened the folded paper with apprehension. Her eyes re-read the message over and over again whilst attempting to make sense as to what it said. *Harriet Beecher, Ralph Waldo, Michelangelo. Spell the last for their answer to all unknown.*

Her brain wrapped itself around for a spell, trying to decipher what the sender was driving at in its intent. She decided to visit Walter at the bank about the note and headed straight there, wishing for a break from the sun on the sidewalk. The clerk informed her that he was in his office with someone else at the moment, but offered her a chair by the door to wait. Since the door was not constructed out of a thick wood, the voices from within the room became audible to her ears as both their tempers increased.

"I cannot believe she just left you by the tree. Oh, and we need to discuss the other matter then."

"Fine by me. But you better believe it. Because it is the truth. And you owe someone five dollars, as I recall."

Murial's face reddened with anger and her volcanic temper drove her to bulldoze her way into the office, stunning Jack and Walter with her inopportune appearance. "HOW DARE YOU! I knew I was right about you. Things do not change much, do they?" Before everyone in town caught wind of all of the commotion, Walter slammed the door shut behind Murial as she kept shouting. "You played me for a bet! No REAL gentleman would do that!"

"And no REAL lady would eavesdrop on a conversation on the other side of a closed door!" Jack countered.

Walter tried keeping the peace between them in vain; sorely losing and slumping into his desk chair as the two cannons fired at one another in a barrage. Only when they had run out of insults to shout at each other, did Walter take the chance and allowed himself back into the argument.

"Wow, a solid twenty minutes! Now, if we have that out of the way…" He replaced his pocket watch back into his vest pocket and made sure he had Murial's undivided attention. "Murial, my dear cousin, you need to stop this madness. I placed a bet with Curt, his Deputy, that Jack would not tell you the truth in order to get him to come forth and thus tell you." Murial's eyes softened a shade. "Now, why don't you give him a chance, hmm?" Her cousin cast a challenging look in her direction.

Murial peered around Walter to size Jack up. She didn't say anything, bringing the note up in front of Walter's face with the written message visible. Her cousin took the note over to his desk in puzzlement. "What does it mean?" Walter turned to Jack who also approached the desk to see for himself.

"I don't know. That is why I am showing it to you." Murial stood on the opposite side of Jack, with Walter in the middle, and the threesome studied the wordage for ten minutes. They took turns spouting out possible ideas before Jack had to go on duty. Walter handed him the five dollars for Curt and handed the note back to Murial.

"Sorry, Murial. I just don't get it. Last thing we need is a riddle of names."

Murial's eyes lit up brighter than a Christmas tree. "THAT'S IT!" She exclaimed, grabbing the note and pencil from Walter's hand, and returning it to the desk. Underneath the singular lined message, she wrote down the last names of each of the corresponding people and read them aloud to Walter. "Stowe, Emerson, and Buonarroti."

"Okay, now what?"

"Do you not see it?" Murial spoke each of the beginning letters as she underlined them. "S...E...B" she turned around to find Walter's mouth hanging open.

"I don't believe it." He softly stated, still staring at the answer as if it were an amazing magic trick.

"It has something to do with Uncle Seb's death. I know it does." She was about to rush out the door when her cousin stopped her. "What? We have to tell Jack about this." Her excitement was slightly deflated when she saw Walter's eyes.

"Let me do it." He forced a smile and Murial reluctantly gave him the note. Her intuition told her that something was up and it was better for her to stay out of it for the time being.

As she exited the bank, her mind was preoccupied with the revelation of the note and she failed to notice a man hunched over a barrel, watching her from the side alley. The taller man sported a well-groomed mustache that clashed with his haggard outerwear and a hat with a singular brown feather stuck through a woven band. His hand produced a match from his pocket and he struck it aflame by the side of the barrel of trash. A hand-rolled cigarette rested on the edge of his parched lips and he drew a couple of smokes before dropping the match into the barrel. As the man's new spurs glistened under the sunlight, he strutted away from the fire engulfed barrel starting to work its way toward the powder kegs resting beside it.

Murial was halfway toward Molly's, for a late lunch, when her ears were rocked by the sound of wood exploding. She jerked herself around in time to see shards of wooden planks being catapulted into the air as the bank caught on fire. Fear drove her madly back down the street, praying that her cousin was not killed by the blast.

To the left of the bank, a neighboring building housing Mr. Rodskin's Smith Shop was also lit ablaze. Her eyes were petrified at the sight of seeing the body of the clerk lying motionless on what used to be the bank's front sidewalk. Half of his body had been burned, sliced up by the blast and the wooden debris. The town was descending upon the scene as many of the people were bringing buckets full of water from various water barrels placed throughout the town in case of such an emergency.

Curt gathered Murial up in his arms, who was still running over to reach the bank, and was fighting against his restraint. "Please Miss Robertson, stay here." She paused her flailing arms long enough for the Deputy to think she was obeying his request and at the moment he released her, she raced away from him.

Men and women were creating human chains to carry the water more efficiently as Murial just stared at where Walter's office had been moments before. Parts of his chair were lying in the middle of the street and she cried when she recognized the pocket watch partly hidden by the seat. It had been dinged and covered in blood splatter. She fell to her knees and buried her face in her hands. Her voice was speaking out in denial of what she suspected while her heart sank into the pit of her stomach.

Glancing around, her eyes located another body that had been completely charred and partially missing. She wanted to scream into the sky but nothing came out of her mouth.

A young girl and boy raced over to her and yanked at Murial until she came with them over to the dress shop. Mrs. Wilkenson, an elderly widow, tried getting through to her, but Murial's mind had stopped comprehending and her ears shut down completely. Her gaze was glued on the bank's remnants and the smoke billowing toward the empty sky while Jack and his deputies were orchestrating the town's efforts to save the rest of the buildings along main street.

Murial stared down at her trembling hands.

Walter...

A cup of tea was cradled between Murial's fair-skinned fingers, but it remained untouched. The warmth on her palms reminded her of back home, around the fire with the family during Christmas ten years prior. Their Grandmother was teaching Walter and Murial how to play chess. As the fire's comforting glow pulsed on their faces, its light seemed to bring the marble chess set to life. But as a young Walter's cheerful face came into focus, her head shook the memory away.

The fire destroyed five of the buildings in the line, though two of them had been thankfully deserted. Only one other proprietor had suffered, Mr. Jenkins and his saloon. He had just received a fresh supply of liquor and all the new fuel for the fire doomed his business. Everyone was exhausted and some of the ranchers, who had been gathered up by one of the young boys, just arrived to help the weary townsfolk clean up the mess.

Murial picked herself off of the sidewalk in front of the dress shop in time for the young boy, from earlier, to hold his hand out for her. She looked down at the blackened pocket watch in his small palm. Tears streamed down her cheeks and she gently picked the busted timepiece up. Bending down to give the child a hug as a thank you, she caught a glimpse of Jack walking toward her.

She rushed over to him and threw her arms around his neck, practically jumping at him. They embraced for a long time, her grip not wanting to let him go. "Murial…" Jack began.

"Don't. Do not say it. Please do not say it." Her eyes were tightly shut. "He is gone, isn't he?"

"I am so sorry, Murial." Jack gently pried her off of him and led her away from the commotion. "My deputies can handle this. Let me take you back to the hotel." Murial rejected the idea.

"I should help with the clean-up. I have been such an invalid, not doing anything and just watching everyone else helping." She tried to turn back, but Jack kept her from returning.

"Murial, its okay. We have enough hands at work." Her body felt heavy; however, she refused to sulk alone in a hotel room and suggested going back to the edge of town where the trees were peacefully standing by the stream. Jack agreed and the two walked silently down the street.

A small breeze had picked up and brushed through her hair as Murial sat on a flat rock beside Jack. She stared into the distance, watching the clouds' shadows paint a patchwork landscape beyond the hills. Her thoughts were calming down and she peered over at him. "I have been so rude. He was your best friend, Jack. I am so sorry." She placed her hand on his.

"Thank you, but you haven't been rude, Murial. We are both still in shock." Jack wrapped his fingers in between hers. Silence took them over once more as they gazed out over the land, finding comfort in just being in each other's company.

The next six days went by slowly for Murial, who had turned to her artwork as a way of dealing with her grief. Jack took the afternoon to evening shift most days, but would stop by for dinner whenever he could. They utilized some of the time together in order to devise a plan that would incorporate her father's bodyguards into a successful twenty-four hour surveillance. While Murial normally despised being one of her father's workhorses, she was grateful to have something to do. She thought about Walter's last request to her and decided to give Jack a second chance. Over the next few days, they had grown a little closer, but her father's eventual arrival nagged at the back of her mind.

Being next of kin, she had overseen the funeral arrangements with the help of Jack and Curt. The undertaker walked her through the process he normally performed and designed a beautiful box for her cousin's partial remains. The preacher presided over the freshly dug grave while most of the town stood in attendance. Murial had a black dress made by Mrs. Wilkenson's dress shop and her body sweated something awful underneath the heavy fabric. She thanked the preacher for his service and watched the younger lads begin shoveling the dirt on top of her cousin's box. As she watched the wildflower, her hand had thrown down the hole during the service, disappear under the rocky soil, her eyes welled up with the realization once more.

That evening was uncharacteristically chilly for the town and blankets were running scarce. Jack and Murial sat together by the window, looking upon the snowcapped mountains in the distance. Her eyes followed along the folds in the blanket she had draped over her lap. "My father is not going to be happy seeing you again." Jack didn't say anything. "What are you going to do if he gets into one of his moods?"

"My job." Was all that Jack said. Murial decided not to press the matter any further and just rested her head on his shoulder as he put his arm around her. Part of her didn't want to ask the questions looming in the back of her mind, fearful of what the truth might entail. But, the other part of her was determined to find out what was going on. Regardless of how close the two of them had become over the last week, Murial could not help but feel like Jack was holding something back from her. At various occurrences, he would be secretive about where he was or who he was meeting with. One time she managed to catch a glimpse of a man in the shadows before he turned away.

When she had asked about it before, he would simply tell her that it was part of his investigation into Walter's death. The powder kegs used for the explosion had left behind a circular pattern that gave way to their location. An eye witness account revealed the presence of the mysterious man that had been watching Murial from the alleyway. Jack and his deputies were hitting dead ends in all other aspects, although that didn't stop him from tirelessly searching. He had been surviving on such little sleep the past two days that Murial would not have been surprised if he passed out from pure exhaustion. The uneasiness of her thoughts gave way when she heard Jack's voice.

"I was thinking Murial that…" he hesitated, not sure how to word his next line. "That if whoever is targeting your father has him scared, then maybe you should head onto California in advance, to be on the safe side." Murial could not believe what her ears had heard him say.

"Jack, are you trying to get rid of me?"

"No, no. That isn't it. But Murial, I do not want you to get caught in crossfire or anything…and your father would not want that either."

"I do not care what my father thinks."

"You keep saying that, but I know that is not entirely true. Despite the facade you put on, you still long for his approval."

Murial looked down at her hands as Jack's fingers interlocked with her own. "While that may be true, you know better than anyone here, except for Walter," her voice broke off before continuing, "that I can handle myself and have seen more gunslingers fight it out than I have been to social events. I'm staying and that is final."

Jack's weary face smiled. "I had a feeling you would say that, but it was worth a try."

Suddenly the answer to the mysterious message resurfaced in her mind. With everything else that happened, she had forgotten all about it. "Jack, I forgot all about the note." She informed him on how the last names spelled out Uncle Seb's name and her theory that his death had something to do with what was going on currently. Jack was surprisingly silent at her idea. "What do you think?" She tried prompting him to make some sort of response.

"I think I need to get some sleep."

Jack was about to get up when Murial stopped him

with her words. "Jack, there is something I have not told you." Regret gnawed at Murial from the inside. She had been wanting to tell Jack a secret she promised to hold for her father. It was information pertaining to the person, or persons, that was behind her father's fear. But her strange loyalty to him had prevented her from saying it to anyone, not even to Walter.

"Don't tell me…you are already engaged?" Jack humored.

Murial couldn't help chuckling. "No, it has something to do with the threats my father received. He promised me to secrecy, but…" Jack glanced over at her while she hesitated. "Well, I'm not quite sure what to make of it. He had shown me one of the threatening letters and it said 'You will be hunted down like the prey you once thought me of.' And it was signed 'The Serpent.'"

Jack's reaction gave Murial cause to be concerned as he appeared to be pushing back an idea that surfaced in his mind. She tried to press him for an explanation. "What? Do you recognize the name?"

"I heard your father call someone that a long time ago. But it can't be the man I am thinking of because…" Just then, the hotel clerk knocked on the door and informed them that the Senator had arrived.

Murial and Jack exchanged stunned faces at the early arrival of her father. Her mind tried gathering all the strength she could muster and Jack offered to go downstairs to greet the Senator. "That is sweet of you; however, you should get some rest." Her body leaned in closer to his and she kissed him on the lips. Abruptly, she moved backwards and apologized. "I'm sorry." Jack brought her back toward him and kissed her in return.

"Do not apologize; I have been waiting a long time to do that." They embraced in a hug and Jack whispered in her ear. "You cannot allow him to dictate your life, Murial. You need to let him go and live your life your way." Her heart felt like it was finally beginning to heal, as if floating on air. Jack's hand gave Murial's a gentle squeeze for encouragement as they separated in the hallway and she took in a deep breath before descending down the stairs.

Her stomach churned as she saw her father standing by the hotel door, the light from the lanterns illuminating the highlights of his worn out, light-colored face and ragged beard. She took a second look to see if it was the same man she left behind over a week ago, his appearance having aged immensely since her last encounter with him. His eyes were strained from weariness and his hands fumbled with his grandfather's pipe as he brought it to his lips, trembling. A deep and cracked voice cut through the still darkness.

"There you are. Took your time getting down here to greet me."

"This is a surprise, Father. You were not due to arrive just yet and the hour is getting late." She took a step backwards when she noticed his eyes hardening their stare on her.

"Yes, I do know what hour it is and you must think me blind, Child. Who was that in the hall with you?"

"Just someone expressing their condolences over Walter's passing, Father." Murial hoped that he couldn't read through her lie while some smoke puffed up from the century old pipe in his mouth.

"Poor Walter…he was a good man." Senator Robertson swung around his left hand in a great display of a mostly emptied bottle of gin he had been carrying in his pocket. Murial's eyes rolled as she scolded herself for not recognizing he was under the drink again.

"Father, I believe some rest is in order. We should get you checked into a room." She reached out to touch his arm only to be refused with flagrant dismissal. He had turned around to survey his bodyguards by now and Murial silently pleaded for her father to go to his room without much fuss.

"Nonsense, we have to drink to Walter."

"You have already done that Mr. Robertson, seven times already." Clive weaseled his way out of the stagecoach and into the main lobby of the hotel. Murial squinted her eyes as she was trying to distinguish in the poor lighting what was wrong with his face. She had to suppress a giggle when she saw that he had a blackened eye.

"Clive, what happened?!"

"Nothing." His pride was still hurting, so she guessed it was fresh, but he tried covering up his wounded ego by taking care of the room arrangements. Murial gave the four guards instructions for the night before heading back to her room. She was grateful to her father's drunken state for clouding his eyesight but dreaded what the next morning would bring. When her head hit the pillow, she fell asleep almost instantly for the first time in her life.

Murial finished making her hair up when her father knocked on the door to her room. "Come in!" She shouted as she placed the last loop of her brown hair around a bobby pin. His face was shielded from the morning light by his hands while he made his way over to her.

"I must apologize for the state I was in last night, Murial. A little too much whiskey I am afraid." He coughed into a fisted hand and straightened his jacket.

"I think you mean gin, Father." She dryly corrected. His tongue licked his right hand to slick his hair back in a more civilized manner. "Where is your hat?" Murial sassed.

"Do not be giving me any of that attitude, Daughter. I may have not been in a complete right state last night, but I was coherent enough to remember what happened."

Murial closed her eyes and took a deep breath, the fight about to commence. "And what pray tell did happen Father?"

"There was a man in the hall with you."

"I already explained that the gentleman was only conveying his condolences. Now, what happened? You should be at Minerstown."

"After receiving your telegram about Walter, we decided to come straight here. Where are we anyways.... Coble...Constan...uh...."

"Conestone."

"Right, Conestone. I have instructed Braden that you are to remain by my side at all times during our stay here."

"What?!"

"After what happened to Walter, I want you under protection and the easiest way that my men can do that is if you stick with me."

"Father, the sheriff and I have already gone over your security details and we have a..."

"You discussed my security with an OUTSIDER?!" Senator Robertson flew into rage. "Murial, have you forgotten why you are here?" Her mouth opened to respond but she wasn't able to get a single syllable out before her father continued on with his rampage. "My life has been specifically threatened just weeks before your cousin is blown apart days ago, and here you are spreading my secrets to every person you meet!" His unkept hair matched the behavior of the wild man standing before her.

Murial decided to let the matter drop due to her desire of keeping Jack's identity a secret for as long as humanly possible. Her father saw the cogs turning in her head. "What has your mind spinning girl?"

She quickly covered her thoughts by changing the subject. "Do you have your lines prepped for the speech this afternoon?" The Senator was not so easily abated.

"Yes, but that does not answer my question. Your expression just now, something is bothering you."

"Why can't you be like other men and not notice some things?"

"I work in politics where everything has a double meaning, a doubled-edged blade so to speak. One has to notice small differences." He squinted his eyes against the light pouring in on her face. Before he could continue his questioning, Clive knocked at the door and Murial gave him admittance with relief. The blackened eye had swollen since the night before, causing Murial to wince with pity when she saw him.

"Does it hurt much?"

"I have no idea as to what you are referring to Ms. Robertson. If you would not have gone against my opinion of Burkville, in the first place, I would not have had my face altered." He brushed her aside and strolled confidently over to the Senator.

"Sir, we really should meet some of the folks around town before convening for your speech this afternoon." Clive paused and turned back to face Murial. "You have picked a location to house his speech have you not? Or were you too busy to do your job properly?"

Resentment built up like steam in a sauna inside Murial, but she remained calm. "Why yes, Mr. Johnson, I did. Between making dinner and straightening up the parlor, I managed to sneak in some time to work on that."

"Murial, watch your tongue." Her father commanded, still wrestling between the light and his hangover.

"If he can't deal with what he dishes out, then he should not be dishing at all," Murial retorted and left the room before she spouted off any more. Clive eagerly turned his attention to his boss the second she left.

"Sir, I have some information that might interest you." Senator Robertson's eyes hardened as Clive told him the news from the street.

The few clouds in the sky hampered the sun's rays for a couple moments, blocking the light off of Murial as she walked down the sidewalk and turned toward a nearby alley. She had caught a glimpse of Jack's back and moved over in his direction for a chat when she noticed a man in shadow having a conversation with him. With no sunlight in the darkened alley, Murial only saw a sliver of the man that was visible under his sombrero. Like a flash of lighting, he vanished and Jack turned around to face Murial. "Good Morning. How did it go with your father?"

"I was only able to sidestep a few traps because Clive had come to the door with his usual insults." Murial reached out and grabbed his hand. "Who was that?"

"No one. Just someone passing along some information." Jack walked with Murial down the sidewalk and toward the trees, where a banner was already being raised. "Already out campaigning, huh?"

"Yes. He did not even ask me where Walter is buried. They are such a pair...my Father and Clive."

"Is he ready for his speech?"

"He says so." She looked down at the dirt. "Jack, did

45

that man seem a little familiar to you?" Jack continued walking without looking in her direction.

"In what way?"

"He almost reminded me of Uncle Seb, but that cannot be and I didn't get a good look at…" They stopped walking and Jack locked eyes with her.

"Your uncle is dead Murial."

"I know, but…"

"He is dead. We were both at the funeral. He is gone." Jack gave her a kiss on the cheek in reassurance. "Do not worry about it. We just need to focus on making sure your father gets through this alive." She nodded her head and forced a small smile to appear on her face. Her gut did not like Jack's constant secrecy and she excused herself back to the hotel, declining his offer to be her escort.

A gentle breeze was welcomed on her face as her mind swirled and her forehead began to sweat. She stood on the opposite side of the street, watching her father shake the hands of the townsfolk and invited the owners of the three destroyed businesses to attend his speech for a big announcement. While standing there, her ears picked up on a small sound of crunching glass coming from behind. Her body swung around on the defensive to face Clive, grinning from ear to ear.

Murial sighed at the pompous brat and she was ready to let him have it. "I will not be summoned like a dog any more, Clive!" She shouted in his face, a small bit of saliva landing on his cheek. He brushed it off and stared coldly at her.

"Are you done flying off the handle?"

Murial glared in return. "What do you want?"

"You are to join your father for his speech." He smiled. "Remember, you are to be under protection." It gave him some strange delight to see Murial in misery, although

46

she had no idea as to why. Her heels pounded the dirt as she stormed across the street with Clive in tow. She reached her father's fake welcome and smiled for the crowd. The group made their way down to the trees where some of the locals had strung up his political banner. Usually, her spot was to remain two feet behind her father so that he could have the entire spotlight, but this time she was surprised to find her father keeping her beside him.

"Today, I will not just be talking about statehood for this fine territory, but also about one of your own. Walter Crancin was a good man and a part of our family. What happened here cannot go unpunished and I want all of you to know that I will be working with the Sheriff on this matter to catch whoever did this!" The crowd of twenty-five applauded for his statement before he continued. "And I have invited the three gentlemen, who lost their businesses, to please join me up here."

Three men stepped forward while the suspense was hanging in the air. "I would like to offer Mr. Rodskin, Mr. Jenkins, and Mr. Fowler a donation that will cover half of their costs to reopen with no strings attached." Murial was stunned to see such generosity from her father and the crowd cheered for his unexpected kindness.

Murial stood by Clive while her father shook the hands of the grateful business owners. "So, I am sure that our protection detail is caring so much for that little bit. Did you even talk to them before telling him to help the Sheriff?" She asked him under her breath.

"It was not my idea." His response was so undertone that Murial actually believed him. *My father made his own decision?* Suddenly she wasn't feeling so well.

Mr. Renald and Mr. Braden were flanking all three of them on their trip back into town. Murial kept her eyes peeled for anything suspicious like a reflex and her father went about smiling and chatting with the folks along the way. The convoy arrived back at the hotel where Mr. Thompson and Mr. Grady were guarding the entrance and her father headed the convoy up the stairs. Mr. Grady opened the door for the threesome and when her father faced her, the look that greeted her instantly took her back to that New Year's Eve night. She felt her inner energy draining and she slowly gulped as the door swung shut after Clive entered, a smug look growing on his face.

"Jack Fulton?!" Her father's eyes pierced through her and into the next county. She shifted her gaze down at the ground. "Jack Fulton is the Sheriff?! And you have been spending time with him I hear." Murial's gaze remained steadfast and transfixed at a wooden board under her feet.

"Yes, but it was mostly due to Walter's passing and your protection, Father."

"I told that man never to speak to you again. Clearly he did not understand what that meant." Senator Robertson picked himself off of the chair and uncapped a nearby bottle. His hand filled the glass with half whiskey but he stopped himself before it touched his lips. "When will you grow up, Murial?!"

She wasn't sure how much more of the Senator's put downs and Clive's insults she would be able to take. His statement was only met by silence so he continued after a pause. "I was not going to tell you until we reached California, however, I guess now is as good a time as any." The whiskey lured him into a brief sip to steady his shaking hands. "Once we get to California, you are to be betrothed to Senator Drouther's son, Samuel."

Murial was stunned and a fire welled up inside her stomach. Her icy eyes yielded no mercy. "HOW DARE YOU!!" She lunged forward at him, stopping within inches of his face. Clive was already preparing for his defense by flying to the Senator's side.

"It has been in the works for three years now. My standing in the Senate is slipping faster than a mudslide and Senator Drouther is climbing just as fast. He has offered me a deal. In exchange for you to marry his son, and for me to help him turn this territory into a state, he will help me keep my office." Murial fumed with her volcano about to explode on a catastrophic level.

"You are rotten to the core! There is not a ghost of a chance that Senator Drouther picked me out of all of the eligible women 'due to my uncouth nature like a wild animal,' as you like to refer to me."

"Because he sees it as retribution for what my father did to his, it is a long story. Regardless, the point is that it has eaten me alive from the inside ever since."

"Oh, I'm sure it has." Murial sarcastically snapped. "That is why you sent Jack away after he told you about his real feelings towards me."

"I knew before then. The way he looked at you, something you didn't even notice. I have learned that reading eyes can be a great help in reading the desires of people." He stared long and hard into her's. "I could not have him ruin the deal. So I set him up with your sister to deter him, but to no avail."

Her pulse raced in her veins. "All to save your own skin in a world full of backstabbing lies and deceit? I will say, at least you fit in with the rest of them."

"Murial, give me a break. I have been on the wrong side of too many proposals and dealings to keep going on my own power and popularity alone. Drouther picked you because he knows that you are my favorite, as pathetic as it may sound, and knew it would hurt more. Look, I was torn between the two loves in my life...my office and my family. I did what I thought would be the best for both."

"No you did not! You decided what was best for you without giving me a second thought, let alone the rest of our family." Murial's cap had blown off.

"Samuel is a good man and you would be well provided for. Look around you Murial. Look back at all the towns you have seen. A life with Jack would have led here. Scraping by on mere pay and for what? For him to be killed in some shootout and leave you with nothing?"

"Don't you go turning this into something it is not. You are not saying this for my benefit but rather to ease your own conscience, if one remains." Murial turned abruptly and started for the door. Clive stepped in front of her, keeping her from exiting the room. "Get out of my way Clive if you do not want a matching set of black eyes."

"Where do you think you are going?" Her father demanded.

"Anywhere but here."

"I don't think so. This deal must go through, or I will be finished in the Senate."

"That is not my fault, nor my concern!" Murial attempted to bypass Clive who restrained her by grabbing her arms and pulling her back toward the table where her father was standing.

"You do not understand Murial. We will be left destitute if I lose my position."

"Why should I care about your failure with money? It is my life, not yours being sacrificed like meat on a platter - carved up for the highest bidder." Murial tried shaking herself free from Clive's grasp but ultimately resorted to jamming the heel of her boot into the notch where his ankle joined his foot instead.

Clive winced in pain and released his grip enough for her to race to the door, swing it open and dash down the hall before her father's bodyguards had a chance to get up from their poker game. She dared not look behind her as she plowed her way down the stairs and out the hotel door as the sound of her father cursing at his bodyguards resonated from the second floor.

Murial ran as fast as she could across the road and past all the shops in town. Her sense of direction was lost, in more ways than one, but that didn't stop her from racing away from everything. The sun blinded her eyes, though she kept moving forward despite not being able to see what was in front of her. Not until she was forced to stop for air did she even consider the notion of resting. Drying out under the rising heat, her eyes surveyed the area around her, looking for a source of water. She felt a flood of relief crash upon her when she noticed an old well by a thriving tree in the near distance.

The rocks creating the well's walls were crumbling with age, but still stood their post. Murial threw herself against the wall and eagerly peered down the darkened hole, listening for the rush of water her ears were longing to hear. Nothing. Her eyes closed and she strained to hear the water she hoped would be there. "There is nothing down that well."

Murial's eyes flew open and she spun around to see a poor white woman approaching her. Her clothes were faded but not torn and her hair was pinned back in a perfect bun. No shoes adorned her feet and her hands were calloused from hard work. "What you seek is not there."

"What do you think I seek?" Murial quipped.

"Water. Why else would you come to a well?" The woman stepped closer to Murial but still kept her distance. "I think you are lost, child."

Murial was too exhausted to argue with the lady, and her sides heaved while trying to recover from her escape. "I think I am too."

"If you would like to rest under that tree, feel free to do so." The woman gestured with her right hand toward the tree approximately four feet from the well's side. Murial took her up on the offer without hesitation.

"Where do you live?" She asked the stranger.

"In a hut not far. But I suspect you come from much farther away."

"How do you know that?"

"You're attire and mannerism. Besides, no one from these parts ever comes up here." A smile dawned on the strange woman's face, revealing some wrinkles by the corners of her eyes. Murial chuckled and invited the woman to sit down next to her under the shade of the tree.

"So, what are you running from?" Murial admired the directness of the stranger.

"My father." Her answer did not satisfy the woman.

"And?" Murial gave her an inquisitive look, to which the woman simply replied, "no one runs like that merely from a family situation. Perhaps you were running from something else? Yourself, for instance." Murial's eyes looked down at her hands kneading themselves over and over again. She pondered how this stranger could be so insightful after having just met her.

"I guess you could say that." Murial fought with the tears forming. "It is like I have been in a choke hold with no way of escaping the forever tightening squeeze of a snake."

The stranger placed her hand on Murial's shoulder to comfort her. "I think I understand the concept. You are breathing, but not really living."

Murial couldn't keep the flood gates closed and a tear managed its way down her cheek. She tried covering it up with a swipe of her hand and forced a smile onto her face, but she knew that the woman was not fooled. "I'm sorry."

"For what? For being human? There is nothing to apologize for, Miss. Sometimes we need to break down before we truly heal." The woman's smile was compassionate and Murial felt safe in her presence. "You may rest here a few more minutes, but you must return to town then."

Murial's fear mounted. "I know that I must face my fear, but I am not sure if I will have what it takes Ma'am. I have been stuck for so long."

"Then I think it is time you break free." The woman picked herself up off the ground and looked down at Murial. "All my life I have found comfort in the beautiful night sky. Gazing up at the stars, everything seemed clear under them. It was like they could read me as if I were a well thought out book. When times grew hard during the day, I would often times wish it was night and I could share my problems with the sky. Many moons ago, I realized that the stars are always there but not always visible. The same way He is always there, but not always seen. Trust and lean on Him for your strength my child."

Murial thanked the woman for her kindness and offered to buy her some shoes from town. The woman was grateful for the gesture, but humbly declined. "I learned that the dirt is going to enter the shoes anyway, so why bother trying to keep it out?"

She watched the stranger leave and took a few moments to savor the tree's shade before heading back to town.

Murial traced her steps back and as she reached the outskirts, Jack raced up to her and threw his arms around her in an embrace. "Are you alright? One of my deputies saw you race out of town but couldn't be sure which direction through the maze of alleys back here. We were about to gather a search party together."

"We?" As if answering her question, Curt popped out from behind an adjacent building and sighed when he saw her in Jack's arms.

"Thank goodness you are safe. We were about to round up some volunteers."

Murial smiled. "I did not mean to cause such fuss." Jack gave her a small kiss on the forehead. They walked back into town while Murial told them everything her father had revealed to her and the two men stared at one another.

"Now that all makes sense. And that also explains the fight your father had with his brother." Jack was beginning to piece the puzzle together.

Murial turned to him, "Uncle Seb?"

Jack nodded. "Senator Drouther, you said? Is he not the son of Thomas Drouther? If I remember correctly, there was a story about your Grandmother and how she was also a deal breaker in a political alliance that helped your Grandfather, and shattered Drouther's father's career in politics."

The story was vague in the back of Murial's mind, and she instantly realized what she had to do, but she still wasn't sure if she would be up for it.

Suddenly, gunshots rang out from the hotel when the building came into their sights, causing the threesome to hunch down while running up to the porch. Jack, Curt, and Murial scrambled up to the second floor of the hotel and cautiously approached the opened door to her father's room. They inched their way against the wall and Jack drew his Single Action Army Colt from his side holster when they came upon four dead bodyguards lining the threshold.

"Murial, go and fetch my other deputies at my office." Jack whispered. Murial sped back down the hall while Curt checked the bodies for a possible pulse. He shook his head to silently let Jack know that none was found.

Murial flew down the stairs and out to the sidewalk. She focused in on the Sheriff's office, but suddenly halted when the sound of spurs came up from behind her. A large, tanned hand clasped over her mouth and an arm wrapped itself around her waist. The bitter taste of unwashed human skin hit her taste buds as her teeth bit down with force on the calloused hand until the man it belonged to yanked it free. Her body continued fighting in protest to his restraint until the sound of a gun being cocked by the temple of her head forced her to stop.

She turned slightly to see a stout man with a Whitney Hartford Dragoon pistol aimed by a steady hand. "Get her off the street. We'll take her back by the alley." Her nose noticed the smell of tobacco on the man behind her and her hair could feel the well-groomed mustache he fondled over.

They forced her behind the buildings and walked her back to the hotel. She desperately looked around for something to grab or a way to free herself. Noticing the neck of a broken glass bottle lying on the ground, she faked a fall and scooped it up in her hand as the man hauled her up.

Tucking it away in the pocket of her skirt, Murial heard the slight 'ting' it made when it collided with her Uncle's star and hoped they did not also hear the sound.

The back stairs were rickety and full of weak spots, causing them to take twice as long as it should have to carefully climb their way up, until they reached the back door and threw her into the hall. Jack and Curt were shocked to see Murial standing there when the other men entered in behind her.

She was shoved up against the wall as her father's voice shook with pleading in his messages to someone in the room, something she had never thought her father capable of until now. "Please, Seb, I'm sorry."

"Shut up! Where is your weasel of a manager, Clive?"

"At the General Store. Gathering up people for another speech."

"Getting ready for another sermon of empty lies you mean. How can you talk of freedom when you enslave all around you when anyone defies your beliefs?!"

Murial was shocked; her stomach turning and her mind spinning with the impossibility that it could be her uncle standing in the room, threatening his brother's life. Just then, a crack in the floorboards alerted her that someone was coming up from behind Jack and she tried motioning to them from where she stood.

Curt and Jack turned just in time to see Clive knock them out in a single motion. Holding his Winchester Yellow Boy rifle across the barrel, the butt hit Curt in the forehead just as the barrel's end of the gun struck Jack in the same location. Clive jerked his head toward the room and the two kidnappers thrusted her into the open doorway.

Her mind was trying to comprehend the scene before her in the room. Senator Robertson was on his knees with a familiar Remington Army Revolver pointed at his head by a tall man with a poncho and sombrero. It was the same man she had seen Jack talking to in the alleyway and the same man she recognized from her past. The words were slowly coming forth from her lips. "Uncle Seb?"

Her uncle's steely eyes softened when he saw her. "Murial? Wow, have you grown." His face took on a hint of pride as he spoke but some wriggling on her father's part shifted his attention back to the situation at hand. Clive pushed her forward into the room, shoving the Winchester into her back.

"Nice to see you again, Seb." His words slithered out over her shoulder. The two kidnappers filed in behind their boss, hands at the ready to draw when needed.

"I can't say the same about you, you slimy rat." Seb kept his eyes on everyone in the room. "Shut the door behind you. I don't want any more visitors." Clive kicked the door shut and Murial winced as she heard her only means of escape slamming closed.

"Now, Seb. What are you going to do? The next move is your's." Footsteps pounded up the stairs, announcing the arrival of Jack's deputies investigating into the gunshots.

"Uncle Seb, why are you doing this? How are you alive?" Murial pleaded for some kind of explanation that she knew would not come from her father nor Clive. Her two kidnappers stood on either side of her as Clive positioned himself opposite Seb.

"There is no way you are going to leave this room alive." He cradled the gun in his hands, keeping his stance slightly widened, watching Seb's body language.

"Because you are looking at the man who hired Jack to kill me." Seb smacked the Senator in the head with the butt of his revolver. Murial was sick to her stomach.

Everything she had known about her life was unraveling, even Jack had not mentioned that detail to her in his full confession.

"WHAT?"

The Senator groaned and clutched his forehead with his left hand. "He never told you?" Seb steadied the Remington as he stared down the barrel at his brother, cramped on the floor. "Can't say that I am surprised. After Jack told him that he liked you, threatening to ruin his precious deal for his job, he gave Jack an option. Either never speak to you again or to kill me in exchange for a chat with you. Knowing that my sorry-excuse-for-a-brother would not hold his end of the bargain, Jack came to me. We thought up my death and my brother kept his word the way he always does, in half truths."

Now the funeral made more sense for Murial. She had wondered why Jack had attended the funeral after his sudden disappearance, and even after his explanation, the pieces didn't all click into place until that moment. Murial directed her next question toward her father. "You mean that you let Jack come to the funeral to pay his condolences to me as his reward for killing your brother?!" Her father did not respond.

"Go ahead, tell her!" Seb ordered and cocked the revolver in his hand, watching the Senator's sweat drench his face and beard.

"Okay, okay...yes, and then I told him to leave or I would tell the authorities that he was the one who killed him." Murial found herself wanting to kill her father at this point, joking to herself that she might want to get in line in order to do so.

"Why did you want Jack to kill Seb?!"

"Because I was becoming more popular in the political realm than he was, isn't that right Gerald?"

Murial's father looked at Seb with resentment flaring in his eyes, but Seb continued. "He was always such a greedy pig who hungered for power. I even gave it all up, to become a sheriff, but that did not satisfy him enough because I was still around."

The Senator spit on Seb's shoes and snarled with jealousy. "You know the real reason, Serpent."

Clive was growing impatient. "Enough talking, Seb." But Murial wasn't finished with her questions.

"If you have been alive all this time, where have you been?" By this time, pounding ensued on the locked door by Jack, with Curt and his deputies backing him up.

"It's Sheriff Fulton. Open up. Murial? Clive? Seb, are you in there?" The tension thickened between the six of them, the standoff about to reach its boiling point. Murial's hand reached into the pocket of her dress and grasped the piece of broken glass. Clive ordered the two men to get Seb, brushing past Murial as they inched their way forward. Seb jammed the gun tighter on the Senator's head. "Come any closer and he is dead."

Murial reached her hand up and around the stout man's neck, slashing his throat across his jugular. Blood gushed as the taller man with the mustache turned and drew his pistol at the same moment Seb shot it out of his hand. The stout man's body lay limp on the floor by Murial's feet, his blood pooling on the wooden floorboards.

Clive pointed the Winchester in her direction, cocking it and motioning her to drop the glass. "Brewer, you lied. You told me you were fast." Clive glared at the man with the mustache, pushing Murial to the ground and mirrored Seb in pointing his gun at the back of her head. "If you shoot Senator Robertson, she is also dead."

The pounding ensued and Murial watched the birds flying outside the window in front of her, silently praying as she studied her uncle.

Seb's eyes shifted between his brother and Murial. His hand was shaking slightly and Murial could see him wrestling with the decision he had to face. Suddenly, Clive raised his gun and shot the Senator straight through his forehead. Blood sprayed everywhere on the far wall and all over Seb's clothing. Seb shot Brewer to free Murial, who was in utter shock and Jack busted the door down just as Clive shot Seb in the chest.

The campaign manager shifted his attention to the sheriff, but as soon as he pointed his gun at him, Jack shot Clive down before he could pull the trigger. Curt and the deputies poured into the room and checked for pulses on each of the bodies, finding one on Brewer and no one else.

Murial rushed over to her uncle, bypassing her father's limp form, and grabbed his hand. Blood was seeping from the corner of his mouth and was oozing onto the floor from the wound. Jack instructed one of his deputies to fetch the doctor before kneeling down beside Murial.

Seb gazed up into Murial's saddened eyes and spoke with his weakening energy. "You look so beautiful." A smile spread under her tears.

"You always were a flatterer."

He coughed up some more blood and stared at Jack who shook his head. "I told you to wait for me, Seb. That we would take him together."

"Couldn't have your life ruined, Jack. Besides, I was already dead." He chuckled before the cough took over once more. Tears were streaming down Murial's cheeks.

"Uncle Seb, please…" She couldn't finish the plea her heart desperately wanted to say aloud, not with knowing that it was impossible, given his state. Her uncle read her mind.

"I can't, my little fighter. If you could look inside

my coat pocket…there is something I would like you to have." She felt for the pocket and grasped a necklace with her left hand. When she pulled it out, she saw that the pendant was of a sword and helmet. "A reminder to never stop fighting."

Her lips pursed together while she fumbled with her dress pocket trying to produce her uncle's sheriff star. "See? I have kept it ever since the funeral." She forced a smile and placed it in his hand, folding his fingers over it.

"You're free now, my…." Seb's eyes rolled backwards and his head turned to the right as his last breath left his body. Murial wept as Jack placed his arm around her stone cold shoulders full of despair. Grief consumed her mind and the world stopped at that moment.

It had only been three days since the incident, and Murial was already growing tired of wearing black. She did so out of respect for her uncle but it didn't help raise her spirits when she looked down at the constant reminder she wore. Some of the events still seemed unreal to her even after witnessing it all with her own eyes. Her body was worn and ached from sleep deprivation, caused by the nightmares she had about killing the stout man.

Jack had helped her with notifying the rest of her family by telegram and she wondered how her relatives would be taking it back home. She figured that they would be in mourning for the wrong brother, though she did not care. Her trunk was sitting beside the door, waiting for her like the key to a new world. For the first time, she would have freedom from under her father's tyrannical reign.

The day before, Jack informed her about some letters his deputies had unearthed among Clive's possessions. They revealed his own double-crossing scheme with Senator Drouther in an arrangement eerily similar to that of her father's deal with Jack. Clive had somehow learned of Seb's fake death and used him as his scapegoat for the assassination plot. But they guessed that Clive hadn't counted on Murial spoiling the plan by going to Conestone, instead of Burkville, and Jack alerting Seb to her father's arrival.

Brewer was at the doctor's, recovering from having Seb's bullet extracted from his shoulder, but was put on trial the following morning after the incident. Judge Morgan had wanted to handle the matter rather quickly, given the situation and the severity of the crimes, and Murial had given her testimony as best she could.

Jack walked in and saw her sitting on the edge of the bed, staring at her hands. "Nightmare again?" He asked. She nodded in reply.

"I guess I should not be such a soft-horn, but I have never killed anyone before." He sat down beside her.

"Murial, I still have nightmares sometimes of the men I have killed. In particular, my first one. He was the very man I looked up to and even though it was staged, it changed him. Part of me will always feel somewhat responsible for that."

"It's not your fault, Jack. He decided to do it under his own free will." Her lips displayed a small smile. "I do not blame you, and neither does Seb."

Jack grabbed her hand. "Are you ready?"

Murial rose up from the bed and they made their way to the cemetery for three more burials. They circled around three freshly dug holes, with Walter's in the middle. Uncle Seb was placed on Walter's right while her father and Clive were placed on his left. There were not many in attendance this time around since only a few knew her uncle.

Curt and the deputies stood behind Jack and Murial, being there for her and Seb. The preacher gave a sermon and tried providing some comforting words to Murial before the undertaker started covering the graves. "I hope that we are not to meet under such dark circumstances next time my dear." The preacher shook her hand and nodded to the deputies as he headed back to the church.

After the service, Jack hitched up a small wagon to gather Seb's belongings from his shack in the hills. It took them two hours to reach the little, wooden box for shelter and their words failed them when they saw a person waiting there for their arrival. Murial's face filled with joy when she recognized the rotund gentleman and jumped down from the wagon, rushing over to her cousin.

"Walter...you are alive!" They hugged as Jack came up and took his turn at greeting his best friend.

"So if you are alive, then who is the man we buried under your name? Jack inquired.

"I do not know. Right as you left, Murial, Seb bolted through the back door and dragged me out before the explosion happened. He saw a man outside start a fire with some large powder kegs next to it and grabbed me in the nick of time. He hid me out here and told me to stay until the smoke cleared. Seb said that if I was out of the way, he knew that Murial would turn more towards you, Jack, and he needed to get her away from her father so he could do what he had to do."

Walter's voice lowered. "He also said to give you this when you arrived." He slid his hand into his vest pocket and produced a folded paper that he gave to Murial. She fingered it open and glanced over at Jack before reading it.

Dear Murial,

I will most likely be dead by the time you are reading this. My only hope is that I have accomplished what I have set out to do and you are free to live your life now. A day has not passed when I have not thought about you these past three years. While I have enjoyed Jack and Walter's company, I miss your smiling face and your "full of life" attitude.

All my possessions are your's. Though it is not much, may it help you begin a new life with Jack. I know that you have had your reservations about him before, but he is a good man who loves you almost as much as me. You are lucky to have him.

> *With All My Love,*
> *Seb*

P.S. Is it that time already?

Murial's face displayed her contentment and she thanked Walter for keeping his word to Seb. He informed them that Seb had already packed up his belongings to make it easier for transport and they entered inside to begin loading up the wagon.

The interior of the shack was far different from what the outward appearance would have suggested. It was clean and tidy with his bags lined up on the bed. A cot was jammed in on the other side for Walter, between a small table and the far wall. On the same wall, a beautiful clock rested in prominent display, perfectly placed to be seen as soon as they opened the door.

Her eyes lit up when she recognized it as her Grandmother's clock. It had been passed down to Seb, per her request, when his mother had passed. It was handcrafted and over two hundred years old. Murial headed straight for it, remembering what the letter had mentioned about time and she unhooked the clock, revealing a key dangling from the nail. A piece of paper had been tucked into the clock's back and she could not believe her eyes when she saw the amount written on it.

Walter and Jack peered over her shoulder, stunned at the amount that a bank in San Francisco had under his name. All the information was there, including an address for an old family home back East that the key opened. "I remember now, it's the old farmhouse down Trundle Road. Congrats Murial." Walter gave his cousin a hug and started loading Seb's things into the wagon. "That gives you the clean start you always wanted."

Jack went about assisting Walter and left Murial in the shack, staring after him. Her hand held the key, rubbing her thumb over the groves and thinking back to what her uncle had written down on the letter. She was about to halt Jack before he left with another load of Seb's things to the wagon, but stopped herself short.

The freedom to choose what she wanted to do in life was scary and fear set in where joy had just been. *Amazing how quickly a human heart can change,* she thought. For the first time, she had the freedom to do what she wanted because of her uncle's sacrifice, and at the same time, she could feel the chains of uncertainty enslave her movements. The ride back to town was silent and somber, all three of them watching the landscape with unprecedented attention.

She hadn't spoken much to Jack since the day of the funerals. Her heart felt betrayed at the secret he held for so long from her and she had already been drowning in enough sorrow to last her a lifetime. Jack and Walter had known all the time that her uncle was alive, yet they said nothing. It was most likely her uncle's request for his identity to remain a secret, but that assumption did not make it any easier for her to bear. Murial's hand clasped the stagecoach pass she had purchased in the morning - a one way ticket that would begin her journey homeward, with a side trip in California.

The clock ticked away irritatingly on the wall across from her in the hotel room. Its mechanical increments of time seemed to be pounding away in her ears and she decided to walk away from its infuriating sound. Lost in her own mind, she found herself walking up to the sheriff's office and paused right as her hand touched the door knob. Despite the deception that Jack and Walter had played upon her, she still held feelings for Jack; which made a forever farewell unfathomable.

She walked inside to find Jack at his desk and he rose from his chair the instant she entered the room.

"Murial, it's good to see you. How are you faring?" Jack wanted to give her a hug, but kept his distance out of respect.

"Okay, as good as I can be right now." Murial stood about two feet from him. "I wanted to apologize for ignoring you as of late. I will be leaving on the evening stage tonight. Heading back homeward to Pennsylvania, as a matter of fact."

"No need to apologize. I know that it has been a lot to process, over three years of history all in a single week." He forced a smile on his face for her sake, though his eyes gave away the pain he truly felt. "Before you go, there is something I wanted to give you." Jack bent down to his desk and slid open the top drawer on the left side. His hand reached down and picked up a thick book that he presented to her. It was worn from age and the long trip it endured coming out West.

"Your bible? Jack, I cannot accept this."

"Open it up to your favorite verse."

Murial flipped it open to Revelations 3:8 and gasped when she saw a pressed lilac between the pages, fragile and paled in color. She looked up at him. "Is this the flower?"

Jack nodded and Murial placed the book on the desk before she flung her arms around him. While they embraced, Jack asked her if she would consider staying out in Conestone with him and Walter. Murial pulled her head back so she could look at him as she spoke.

"I have become free in the West, but my life belongs in the East." Jack failed at hiding his disappointment and removed himself from her hold.

"Well, you always have been more tempered for cooler weather anyways. I wish you the best." He wiped his nose with his hand. Murial smiled when she realized he was fighting back some tears.

"See, there was a boy I knew back home. He was a show off and full of himself. Took a fancy to a young girl on his street and did everything he could to get her to acknowledge him, to give himself a chance at making a good impression. And when his time finally came, she treated him like poor dirt. But the boy still loved her and when the time came around again, he came to her rescue." Jack looked over at her with a smile.

"And what happened next?"

"The young girl, a woman now, asked him to come back home with her." Murial's face had not glowed so happy since she could remember, and Jack gathered her up in his arms for a kiss. Her hand held the ticket up for him to see and Jack watched as her thumb slid two more tickets out from behind the first one.

"Two more tickets?"

Walter came busting through the door beaming with pride and Curt followed in behind Murial's cousin. "It only took you two over three years to realize you are perfect for one another. I was acquiring grey hair out there waiting." He chuckled.

"You were spying on us?" Murial teased him. "After I even paid for your ticket and everything."

"Hey, you can afford it now. Without a bank out here, there really isn't much else for me to do. Besides, you are going to need a hand getting that farmhouse back in functioning order." Walter tipped his hat in Jack's direction. Unpinning the star from his vest, Jack gave it one last look before launching it into the air toward Curt, who caught it and smiled at his former boss.

"Going to miss you 'round here. But I do wish you the best of luck, Jack."

"Don't forget to write, Sheriff Ruger." Jack grabbed the rest of his possessions from the desk and headed out the door with Murial and Walter in tow. As Jack went around town to say his good-byes, the other two headed to the hotel and waited in the lobby. Suddenly, Murial remembered the woman she had met at the well and asked Walter who she was.

"What woman?" Murial watched Walter's face growing vexed as she described the location she had visited earlier. "Sounds like you were out at the Old Brown's well, but no one lives out there."

"I know I saw her."

"It could have been the sun playing tricks on you, Cousin. Why? What does she have to do with any of this?"

Murial decided not to tell him about the conversation she had had with the strange woman and changed the subject entirely by asking Walter as to how Uncle Seb obtained his nickname as the "Serpent." Her fingers fiddled with the pendant on the necklace from her uncle as Walter told her about how a younger Seb had gained a reputation of sneaking up on people without making a sound. "As slippery as a snake," he said.

Some curious markings on the back of the pendent caused her to look down at where it lay against her chest, examining the pattern the markings created.

"What is it?"

"My zodiac sign...Sagittarius. It is carved into the back of this pendent that Uncle Seb gave me the day he died."

The clerk on duty at the hotel counter came up to Murial and handed her a telegram from her mother and sister. They shared in her excitement at having her come home and also informing her of the memorial they would have in honor of her father and uncle. By the time Jack arrived with his things, the sun was sinking lower in the sky and he sat down with Murial in the lobby of the hotel. No sooner had his butt hit the seat, than a flash of horses was seen by the entrance as the stage came to a stop at the door.

A group of passengers disembarked from the smelly coach as the driver unloaded the top rack of luggage. His armed guard released the back straps of the rear boot, also containing more of the passengers' belongings, right after handing the bag of mail off to the man in charge of the local post office.

As soon as the passengers emptied out, the threesome gave over their belongings to the driver, and then filed into the coach. Murial clutched her necklace and gazed up at the unseen stars above, silently thanking them for the new life she was about to begin with Jack and Walter.

"So, what are we going to do in California?" Jack asked.

"There is an engagement party that I must attend." Murial's mischievous look caused Walter's eyebrows to rise.

"I like the sound of that."

Another woman soon joined them in the coach and her eyes instantly saw the beautiful necklace hanging about Murial's neck.

"Hello, my name is Heather Brinkshaw. My, that is a very fine necklace you have there. Where did you acquire such a gem?"

"Thank you. My uncle gave it to me. I'm Murial Robertson." Murial smiled, the necklace making her feel as though her uncle was on the stage with them.

As the stagecoach pulled away from the hotel, she thought about how he had always felt more like a father to her, and in fact, she was destined to never discover that he actually was.

<u>THE END</u>

Murial Robertson will be back in...
Angled For Revenge

ABOUT THE AUTHOR:

Sarah Ickes has her Associates Degree in Arts and Design. She has always held a passion for writing since her first publication of a poem in fifth grade. Not only does she persue writing, but she also creates artwork that is available for purchasing, such as the illustrations and book cover of this story. Historical references and topics are a favorite of hers, since she loves learning about history. Please visit her website for more details or follow her on social media.

www.sarahickesart.com

Thank you for reading my novel and I hope you enjoyed it.